About the Author

She has been an avid reader from about the age of ten. She enjoys all the bookish delights the world has to offer.

Bookmarks: An Anthology

Kayla Burns

Bookmarks: An Anthology

Olympia Publishers
London

www.olympiapublishers.com
OLYMPIA PAPERBACK EDITION

Copyright © Kayla Burns 2023

The right of Kayla Burns to be identified as author of
this work has been asserted in accordance with sections 77 and 78 of
the Copyright, Designs and Patents Act 1988.

All Rights Reserved

No reproduction, copy or transmission of this publication
may be made without written permission.
No paragraph of this publication may be reproduced,
copied or transmitted save with the written permission of the publisher,
or in accordance with the provisions
of the Copyright Act 1956 (as amended).

Any person who commits any unauthorised act in relation to
this publication may be liable to criminal
prosecution and civil claims for damage.

A CIP catalogue record for this title is
available from the British Library.

ISBN: 978-1-80439-460-1

This is a work of fiction.
Names, characters, places and incidents originate from the writer's
imagination. Any resemblance to actual persons, living or dead, is
purely coincidental.

First Published in 2023

Olympia Publishers
Tallis House
2 Tallis Street
London
EC4Y 0AB

Printed in Great Britain

Dedication

For my boys, Jackson, Alex and Ben.

Acknowledgements

Thank you to my family and friends for all your support. Dad and Michelle, for their unwavering belief in me. Mom and my boys for being a constant reminder to come back to life. Finally, Brian, for always insisting I am a "grown ass woman" and can do whatever I want.

Emily Do Not Toch

School was out, finally. Emily would miss her friends, but not the homework or waking up early. She would miss the library but opt the weight of her purple tinkerbell backpack, usually with a few more books than she needed.

When her mom picked up Emily and her brother she'd just been flipping through a book from her teacher. There was no inscription or card but it had been given to her with a voiced hope of approval and a few hours of blissful imagination.

The book itself had a blue cover and a handful of chapters about magical princesses.

Emily usually liked princesses and her mother approved of her reading about girls with their own power and ability to use it.

Just as Emily stood to go to her mother's car, her brother grabbed the book and ran ahead. Emily had to give him the advantage since she'd set down her backpack. She tried anyway to run after him with no chance of overtaking him.

In the car, her mother told her to buckle up and for Emily's brother to either read the book or give it back. He made a wrenching sound before tossing the book to her side of the seat. It fell to the floor just out of reach of her booster seat.

Emily thought about crying but was interrupted when

her mother announced they had a stop on the way home. A woman had posted a bunch of crafting supplies online and they were going to pay her a visit.

When they arrived at the woman's house Emily thought it was all just too much. The lawn had actual gnomes and flamingos. Not just pink but all colors. She was allowed to unbuckle and fetch her book then follow her mother to the door.

The woman had invited them to look at some crafts on the patio and talked to Emily's mother about different ribbons and how they could be used to make floral hair accessories.

As they chatted, Emily noticed a thick popsicle stick sticking out from under a table. She pulled at her mother's pant sleeves. Could she have it? The woman had said 'of course' and pondered where it had come from.

An idea had already formed in Emily's mind when her eyes lit upon an open box of markers. It was missing a few but it had a black one, which suited her plan.

Emily looked up at the woman pleading in her expression.

The woman nodded her approval before she distracted Emily's mother with a stack of tiny terracotta pots.

Emily began to write on the popsicle stick.

EMILY

She dotted the I with a heart then drew a larger heart after her name. She added a dot above it and then pulled back to think about what should come next.

DO NOT TOCH

She wrote with the marker to the end of the stick with the final 'h' raised and bent to fit.

Emily looked up at her mother with a mixed feeling of excitement and pride as she blew on the popsicle stick, trying to help it dry. She opened her book and with exaggerated motions placed the stick as a bookmark, still beaming at her mother and the amused woman.

Lidocaine Patch 5%

Bailey usually felt more springy than his 74 years, but the wind January was bringing to his porch made his joints ache. His Marlboro hung between his lips as he sat with his Baldacci novel. The book had been a birthday gift from his daughter the previous June. She'd been out of jail for a few years and had just been starting to accept his attempts at reconnecting. Since June he had read the book three times, bending its spine more with each read. When he stopped he left the book cover up to hold his page without a marker.

As he continued he could hear the news his wife listened to all day. President Bush was announcing airstrikes in Somalia. Steve Jobs introduced a new type of phone. Bailey thought the new phone deal was just a way to make more money, but the airstrikes were interesting. If they actually killed terrorists.

After his Marlboro burned out, he took his book back inside. He could feel the consistent burn on his left side from the leftover side effects of the shingles he'd had the year before.

Bailey tried to hide the wince from his wife, but it was too late. She had already seen it. If he didn't go straight back to their room and apply the damn lidocaine patch he would never hear the end of it.

In their bedroom, the bed was made and one side was neat as a pin. The other side was cluttered with odds and ends that had always seemed a bit much to Bailey. He went to the nightstand and opened a drawer. Inside was a package of lidocaine patches.

Bailey removed one of the remaining two. The second one fell on the floor. The pain in his side was more pressing than the dropped patch. He opened the patch with a knife he'd kept from his army days. After untucking his shirt he applied the patch to the spot of pain on his side. The pain didn't subside immediately, but it would soon. He tucked in his shirt and joined his wife on their loveseat. Book in one hand, his wife's hand in his other.

Together they spent the day reading, watching news and eating spaghetti for dinner. They showered together and she patted his butt like she always had. Two kids and 57 years married they had stayed close and learned how to love each other. Bailey had always been amazed she could love him. She had always said she couldn't ask for a man with more patience.

In bed for the night, they talked about the airstrikes and what it could mean for a country.

They talked of the fancy things people always thought they needed. When she fell asleep he picked up his book and read just a little more.

A cramp seized his arm and he dropped his book to the side of the bed. His eyes lit on the patch he'd dropped that morning. A thought crossed his mind.

Bailey picked up the patch and slid it between the pages of his book. He turned out the light and turned to fall asleep holding his wife.

In Remembrance

It was a Sunday evening when she got the call. Eva Jane had passed away. Her service would be on the twenty second, only six days later.

She didn't owe the family anything, but Eva had been there.

Before she had made the move from Missouri to Idaho, she had been working in a care home. Eva had only been in the home for a few months before the move, but those months had changed her life.

At first Eva's questions seemed harmless. "Pretty ring, he must be handsome to win your hand." "Does he like your cooking?" "Your friends must love him?"

After a while they became; "How did you get that bruise?" "I didn't know you had a house with stairs, are you really being careful with your life?"

Finally they stopped being questions. "You need to leave him."
"He doesn't love you if he hurts you."

Then one day; "What can I do to help you get out of this mess?"

Within the few months they'd planned an escape. The ticket to Idaho and all the things she needed were kept in two suitcases in Eva Jane's room. Smuggled out of her home or given to her by the other ladies in the home.

Eva's daughter picked her up from the care home,

watched her kiss Eva's cheeks. In tears they drove to the airport.

Two years later on an October Sunday Eva's daughter called and once again they would meet at the airport.

At the funeral she was given a card. In Remembrance it said.

In loving memory of Eva Jane. There was a scripture from I Corinthians.

When she boarded her plane home, she tucked the card into a book and thanked Eva for the new life she was given from her kindness.

Blue Symmetry and Windswept

The papers were signed and the moving truck was gone. Jason finally had a place of his own. He walked from room to room, opening boxes as he went. Not that he had many boxes. Mostly books from his old room at his parents.

When he came to the kitchen he sighed. It was a great space and made up for the two small rooms. Lined with new countertops and old but functioning appliances. The only thing he couldn't stand was the color. The tile was white. The counters are a pretty granet. The backdrop, yellow and the cupboards are more orange than yellow.

Jason checked his watch and grabbed his keys. Ten minutes later at the overland Lowes he had six different color swatches in his hands. In the end he'd decided on blue symmetry and windswept. He tucked the swatches in his back pocket and found the rest of the supplies he'd need. When he checked out, he bragged about owning his own place and showed the lady at the counter the colors he had picked. She nodded her approval and moved on to the next person in line.

Back in his truck he slipped the swatches into a paperback for safekeeping. After loading his paint he returned his cart and offered to return the cart of an older man a few cars down.

When Jason returned home, he changed and turned on an audiobook. It was time to prep his kitchen for blue symmetry and windswept.

King County Fair 1995

"You need to be with girls your own age." Jessye's mother had told her.

She had regretted every minute of it. At 15 she was awkward. A little chubby, shorter than the other girls. She was also so socially awkward that when she was picked up all she could say to the parent was 'thank you' and then buckle up. She listened while the other girls talked about boys, and school and summer vacation.

When they arrived, she followed as usual behind the other four girls. In line they were each given a stub off their green admission ticket and a stamp on each hand. Jessye tucked her #165752 inside her book and followed. They fed livestock and played some games. They watched a country boy play some songs about love, heartbreak, and having his truck break down.

Jessye was happy when they started the rides. Each one presented her with a short break from the consistent chatter of the other girls.

In line a boy asked her what she was reading. She held the cover up to his face so he could read it himself and to watch his surprise when she held up a Sci-fi about a boy playing war games in space. He asked questions and she made him laugh when she talked about gravity. They were cut short when the line ended after her turn. Jessye smiled at him and found the last open seat.

The other girls laughed and asked why she didn't get his number. He seemed as awkward as she was. Jessye tried not to watch him as they spun by the line. After the ride though, she met his eyes and smiled again. He waved and the girls were off to the next ride where one of the girls threw up. They decided it had been enough and they wanted a more mild activity.

The girls found a hypnotist. At the far end of the fair. As a group they volunteered.

Jessye ended up laughing uncontrollably at the beck and call of the hypnotist.

When their turn was up Jessye spotted the boy in the crowd, watching her again. She could feel the rush in her cheeks as she followed the girls to the parking lot to meet with their ride.

Later that night, she flipped through her book. The ticket fell to her pillow, she picked it up and fanned her face with it. Jessye thought of the day and the boy she'd talked to about gravity.

Then she set her new bookmark and turned out the light.

Boarding Pass

On January 5th 1984 Mike St. John boarded a plane to Chicago. The weather in Boise was clear and cold but it did nothing for Mike's heavy heart.

His trip would only last a few days, but everything he would miss couldn't be rewound and played again. His oldest daughter would have her first child almost certainly before his return.

Unfortunately, this trip was one Mike couldn't afford to miss. His business had been slowly fading and he needed to learn how to bring it into this modern age.

On Christmas his daughter had gifted him a computer and tickets to a 4-day long convention on how to use it to improve your business.

Snug in his seat, Mike watched the de-icer spray over the wings and wondered if he'd even make it to Chicago. He tucked his boarding pass into his book and closed his eyes, trying not to think of all the things that could freeze and plunge him to a horrible death.

He tried to think about his daughter and the baby girl that would be waiting for him upon his return home. About his wife holding the baby for the first time. About how important the classes would be to the future of his granddaughter. If he made it into this crazy approaching age of technology with a business she could take over some day.

The plane started to move. Mike held his breath. After

a while he grew used to the small turbulence and tried to read a little.

Three hours later he'd finished the book and marked a page at random. He tucked the book into his carry on and met Chicago with a new sense of rightness.

Mini Swiss Quiches

'Boy! If you don't stop now I will END you!" Cassie snarled without lowering her book. Her boyfriend of a year had been pestering her all day to 'go out' and 'socialize'. If he knew how much she had to 'socialize' at work he would give a break. Cassie had one day off and she would be damned if she was going to get up, put on makeup and pretend she didn't feel self-conscious around all the beautiful girls that spent their summer days at the mall. All because her boyfriend wanted to get a pretzel and buy some used games.

Cassie rolled over and finished the chapter before deciding she had to pee, which was dangerous ground. If he thought she was getting up he might try again. Better take the book. It's not like she was planning on using a bookmark on this one. It was a 'day off book.' One she could read all at once if she decided to dedicate her whole day off to its glorious contents.

How many times a day did she wish to be at home, in her underwear, with a book in her lap and a fluffy blanket? Every other minute might be an exaggeration but not by much. Today with the sound of the April rain on her windows, was the day she had fantasized about when she had to spend long hours talking to people about their groceries. When she had to ask over and over how the day was and also pretend her day was just as great.

The next time he asked, she told him it was fine if he wanted to go on his own. She really wouldn't mind not hearing him play CoD in the next room like he had most of the morning.

Cassie took her book to the kitchen, a blanket around her shoulders and made a cup of tea. There was no way she was going to the mall.

When she got back to their room he had made their bed and was tidying up the room. Cassie raised an eyebrow at him and then got in bed with her book. He was visibly angry but said nothing. She finished another chapter and set her book on her lap to watch him. He'd been watching her for the last few pages from the doorway.

"Say it and stop being a creep."

He shook his head and left. At peace with herself and his decision to finally do what he wanted without her. She read another chapter and decided that the rare occasion of having the apartment to herself warranted a bath. Maybe with bubbles, and a face mask, definitely with ice cream.

That meant putting down her book. It was safe now, but the binding was too thick to set open on its pages and have it stay. She really didn't want to ruin the cover. Frowning she looked around until her eyes lit upon an old cooking magazine. She didn't know where it had come from. Cassie opened it to a perforated page and ripped out a recipe for mini swiss quiches. Ten minutes later she was settled in the bath in full self-care mode, absolutely enjoying her day off.

Summer Reading Sale

Robert was going to be late. His date, if she bothered waiting, would probably be disappointed. He was supposed to meet her at the library off Capital. There was some kind of event benefiting the new main library.

He parked and ran in hoping he could still pull off charming, despite his poor start. After a minute he spotted her at the end of a row of tables stacked with books. She was cute, different from her pictures but still cute. Her hair had a pixie cut and a mini skirt. Her black thigh high socks left a small area of skin exposed beneath the hem of her skirt. His heart skipped.

"You're late." was all she said when he stood across from her. She didn't look up from the book she was paging through until she reached the end. After an eternity she closed it and placed it back on the table. When she did look up and smile at him, his heart skipped a second time.

They continued to walk the stacks of books across from one another. Talking about what they'd read or wanted to read. She told him of her hatred of Melville. Robert told her of his love of fantasy and was surprised when she spouted off a list of classic fantasy that she had actually read.

When they checked out they both signed up for the summer reading challenge and he bought her an impressively full basket of books. He asked if he could see her again. Maybe take her to dinner, or a bookstore.

To his amazement she'd said yes and offered a time. She told him to choose the restaurant and bring a copy of his favorite book. Robert walked her to her care and she pulled a bookmark from her bag and wrote down the time and place. She joked that he might consider being on time to the next one. She circled the time three times with a heart.

Robert tucked it into one of the three books he'd bought for himself. She stood on her toes and kissed his cheek. They said goodbye and Robert had a feeling his life had just changed in a beautiful way.

Lime Post-it

In all things in life, Stella was systematic. When she ate, she cleaned the kitchen. When she showered, she dried the tub after to prevent mold. Stella had a system for everything. Even when she read a book she never used a traditional bookmark or random objects like some people preferred. Instead she used post-its. They never fell out and would stick to the outside of the book just as well as inside its pages.

On Tuesday evening, after her shower, Stella changed into her jammies and chose a new book to start. She had just over an hour to read before she had to sleep. The book she chose boasted an epic love story of Tibet. It was hardly two hundred pages. Regardless, she opened the drawer next to her bed and took out a small pad of lime green post-its. Stella set it on top of her pillow and carefully removed the dust jacket, which she carefully set on the nightstand.

Before finally settling into bed, she took her daily vitamins with a glass of water. Her world was blissfully organized. Everything in its place. She was happy. Stella opened her book. There was an inscription inside. Here is to the power of home spirit.

Gallery of Great Things

It wasn't often someone paid for you to go to Hawaii. Dylan knee this was an expensive trip for a wedding he wasn't even important in. It was the last chase his parents thought they'd have to get all the grandkids in one place for a picture. The formal dress was an added bonus.

Dylan was twenty-two, a Spanish and history major at BSU and currently working at a grocery store while sleeping on a futon in his parent's basement. This trip was a serious privilege in his mind.

The first day they'd seen some of the island and then helped set up for the wedding. The second day the wedding party had rehearsals so Dylan had the day to roam. He visited some over-priced gift shops. Tried to learn how to surf and bought a book about a wizard in New York. It looked like part of a series, but that didn't turn him off it.

After a while, he stumbled into a museum. It hosted Hawaiian, Polynesian, and Asian art.

He thought most of it was beautiful and thought seriously about getting a tribal tattoo. It took about two minutes for him to decide it would look misplaced on a scrawny ginger kid from idaho.

Dylan bought a few postcards and a necklace for his mom. He grabbed a flier on his way out that he planned to show his history professor for extra credit. He slid it into his book and made his way back to the hotel to read about a modern wizard detective and not think about the busy wedding day schedule he had the following day.

Borrowed From: 8/23

"It was about time," Arlene mumbled as she looked for some space on her borrowed shelf. She'd loaned a copy of North and South to a coworker months ago and was pretty sure the girl hadn't even bothered to read it. When Arlene asked her what she'd thought her reply was: "it was okay, I guess. I liked it."

'You GUESS!" she thought. You GUESS you LIKE a book as beautifully romantic as Gaskell can write? Maybe the language was too difficult or just maybe, the girl hadn't read the damn book.

Arlene was trying to vent and get over it. Not everyone could have sophisticated opinions on classic literature. She took her 'borrowed from' bookmark and moved it to the front of the book. At the bottom of the same shelf she took a notebook and found the title and the girl's name. Arlene wrote returned next to it and looked over the list. The notebook was full through the fourth page with names, titles and dates of borrowed books. Most of them returned.

Some of the names had asterisks next to them to remind her to never loan books to that particular borrower again. Sometimes they came back water damaged or with seriously broken spines. Once a copy had chocolate smeared inside. Arlene had cried while trying to clean the pages.

After taking a step back she looked over her borrowing

shelf. The books were not all pretty with lather covers or straight spines. Some of them had thrift store stickers. All of the books on her borrowing shelf had touched her soul in a way she needed to share.

Parnassus Books

North 9th street? Jordan hated driving downtown. The address she'd given him was 218 North 9th street. He sighed to himself and knew it was probably going to be worth it.

Everything started two weeks ago. His girlfriend since high school had started planning little hunts for him. She hid notes in little stores where she could talk the employees into playing along. She would text him a time and address and the employees pointed him in the right direction.

The first had been at a pick up at Walmart. The girl behind the counter blushed and gave him a mystery novel. Inside was a note from his girlfriend.

Jordan, I love you.

The second had been at the gas station by his house. When he got a new punch card the back had a note written by her.

Jordan, play my game!

A few days later she gave him a grocery list and told him to shop at the store on Front street. That he had to go through check out 4 no matter what and tell the woman his name.

Then refused to answer his questions. She gave him a letter his girlfriend had written about their first date.

Jordan,
Do you remember our first date? We had lunch together

under the tree in the quad.

Those jocks yelled at us. They called us awful names. Do you remember what you told me? You said it didn't matter what they said. That I was beautiful and it didn't matter what I wore. It didn't matter what was under my clothes. All that mattered was how I felt within them. You were so sweet. Even though my hair was still short then, you picked all the flowers around us and tried to stick them all in my hair. I love you, Jordan. For the way you made me feel then and still make me feel now. Safe and happy with the person I am and the person I am becoming.

I love you.

The next day at work he got a letter from her by way of his boss. The man was usually all business. Somehow, she had got him involved in whatever this was. That letter reminded him of th8ier first kiss. How awkwardly he couldn't get past his nerves until she took his hand.

Jordan,

Do you remember our first kiss? You were so nervous. You walked me home after the dance and we stood at my front door. Your hands were shaking and you kept looking at me and then away. I thought for a minute you were going to break up with me. Looking back, high school is a hard time to decide on our sexuality and you had only just come out. I thought you had changed your mind about me. Then you leaned in. i thought you would kiss me then, but you moved back again. It made me smile and I took your hand. You looked me in the eye and then closed yours. It was the worst kiss ever and I was the happiest girl in the neighborhood.

I love you

What the letter hadn't talked about was the neighbors across the street yelling 'Queer' and how it ended abruptly with her dad opening the door and yelling at them to stop or he would call the police and report a hate crime.

That night, after the grocery store, he came home to a letter from her in the mail.

Jordan,

I love you. The time I have spent with you has truly changed my life. I was so afraid to let the world see me as who I am instead of how I was born. I was also afraid to let the world see. You make me feel safe in a world that isn't ready for people like me. I love the way you make me feel worth being here. I hope from here you will think of what you want with our future. I don't want one without you in it. I want to be with you. Always. I know it was hard for you when you came out. Your parents didn't understand, they thought you needed therapy. You did, but not for your attraction to me, you needed it to learn how to move through the world without the approval of everyone else. I'm proud of the man you are. I'm proud to be your lover and friend. I'm so lucky to have you. That you fell in love with my body then and still love it now, after all the hormones and surgeries. I love you.

Jordan parked outside the Parnassus Books at 218 North street. Inside his girlfriend sat a t a table sipping a cup of tea. On the table was a book. She smiled up at him without saying anything. She pointed at the char across from her.

He sat.

She slid the book across the table from him. Jordan opened it. There was no inscription, but the book mark had something written on it.

Marry me?

Jordan was surprised until he looked up at her. Smiling behind the rim of her cup. They'd been together for six years. They lived together. They had fought what she went through during her gender transformation and still did. She was there when his parents died in an accident out of the country. Why hadn't he thought of this? Obviously, she had done it better than he would have.

She stood and left her chair. Kneeling in front of him, she held out her hand with two rings.

Jordan couldn't breathe. There was only one word. Only one way he felt for her. Only one future he wanted.

All Sales Are Final

Lacy had five minutes before her mom would leave her. She usually was able to push her time in the book section of thrift stores. Today she had five dollars and twelve cents. It was hard to decide which two books she wanted.

Lacy needed two dollars for the bus the next day to get across town to her friends and back. And she didn't have another 6 cents to cover taxes on a third book.

A year ago lacy would have asked her mother to cover it, but she had quit her second job and was making things work. Lacy couldn't bring herself to ask. It was around the same time she had fallen in love with reading. She'd found a classic fantasy series about the dragons and the power of a true name.

She grabbed one of the two fantasy books she wanted and met her mom at the check-out. Her mother raised an eyebrow and asked her if she had enough for both. In February her Christmas money was dwindling and her mother knew it.

It was why she was going to a friend's house the next day. The girl had offered to pay her and give her some old books if she helped color her hair. She wanted a red peek a boo color and lacy thought she could handle that. The books were an old star wars set from the girl's dad which were promised with the condition she read them.

Lucy showed her mom the crumpled five in her palm.

Then she listened to her mother tell her about a lady she worked with that had offered to pay her to dog sit the following Sunday. She knew which dog and refrained from telling her mom the dog would make great jerky.

Instead Lucy agreed to watch the rat dog. As she paid and got her three dollars back she tucked her *all Sales Are Final* receipt in her new book and thought about which ones she would buy after the two jobs were done.

Christmas 1972

The photo had been taken twelve years before in Okinawa, Japan with Mark's sister Melissa and a Japanese Santa. For a while his mother kept the photo on the fridge. They'd only been there to visit their father who had been stationed there for a while longer than originally planned.

Twelve years later Mark himself was stationed in Japan. His mother sent him a small paperback novel with a letter and the picture of his sister and himself sitting on Santa's lap. Mark showed the other men with him including his best friend. Who he was pretty sure had a crush on his little sister. Good thing she was thousands of miles away in Idaho safely away from his charm.

Melissa had liked him since he'd signed up alongside Mark with the marines. He didn't mind but she was too young for the shenanigans his buddy played with girls.

Mark carried the book around during his off time. He'd read it three times but he liked having a little piece of home.

2,4,17,21,30- 38

Today, Sylvia turned 18. She could now legally smoke, have sex with a consenting adult, and buy a lottery ticket. Smoking had never interested her. She didn't have a boyfriend, and the girl she liked wasn't interested in her.

So she bought a Powerball ticket. 4 and 17 were her birth month and day. Her track number had been 2. Her favorite number was 21. 30 and 38 were random for her.

Sylvia had no idea how to purchase a ticket or fill out the slip. The man at the counter rolled his eyes when she told him why she wanted one and asked for help. He did help though and told her happy birthday.

He circled his name on a receipt and told her to find him if she won. She tucked the playslip in the book she'd been given for her birthday.

It was a Sylvia Browne novel her father had gifted her that morning. Her dad liked to give her books by authors with her name. She had wanted to write since she was six.

Now she had the complete works of Sylvia plate, Sylvia day, Sylvia Moreno Garcia and now a start to Sylvia Browne. Her dad had always been supportive in the weirdest ways.

When she told him her preference for girls, he started reading books on how to 'support your gay child' of course he also got a rainvow bumper sticker.

If she happened to win anything good, she'd tip Mr. Eye

roll and buy her dad a rainbow painted boat and live in a fancy hotel while she forced herself to write and live off room service. In her car she set her book on her passenger seat and smiled. Optimism wasn't always part of her character but it was her birthday after all.

Minion

Axel was nine and super excited for the first Friday of the school year. His mom packed a really nice lunch and there was less class time because he also had PE on Fridays.

All day he wondered what game they would play. He hoped they wouldn't have to run on the track. He didn't mind running but he wanted to play.

PE didn't disappoint him. They did both. One lap on the track to warm up and then basketball. The only thing wrong was it didn't last too long before he had to go back to the classroom and sit down again.

He still had an hour left of school after PE. His teacher led them to the library to make sure they were in the system to check out books. There was a new girl in class that had to be added to everything. She seemed really disappointed there was a two book maximum.

Axel was looking for books that had the color dot for his grade when she started talking to him. She wanted to know what kind of books he liked, what he had already read and what he wanted to read. He didn't really like girls but he tried to be nice since she was new.

He didn't know what to tell her. He liked short books with pictures. She showed him a series. It was about a group of people who left a dying earth to live on another planet, but ended up on the wrong planet. He could tell she knew a lot about space and was impressed.

After a while he couldn't think of another reason to not get the book she recommended. He didn't tell her it didn't have a lot of pictures. Axel didn't want to sound stupid. Maybe his mom would read it to him if it was too hard.

She was so excited he got the book. When they got back to the classroom she rummaged through her bag and gave him a small yellow bookmark. It was a little Minion from a movie he watched with his sister. The character looked as happy as she did.

Axel found the first page and read the first line, with a little trouble out loud. After he finished, he looked over the rest of the page and then attached the little yellow bookmark.

"See, I already started it." He beamed at the girl before returning to his desk. Maybe it wouldn't be that bad.

You Have an Appointment On: 9/8 1PM

At 56, Sarah thought she had her diabetes under control. It had been touch and go in her youth. The doctors had diagnosed it late and her parents had struggled to afford the medication she needed.

Sometimes she had to seriously watch her diet to avoid her levels being too high or too low. Once on a school trip a teacher hadn't believed her. She had been told she had to drink the juice. Sarah had almost died when the same teacher thought she was faking an episode.

As an adult she worked to have insurance to afford her insulin. In the 90's testing became easier. The problem at 56 was that despite her best effort, neuropathy had begun to claim her feet. She could bang and kick her heels on the ground and always feel like they had fallen asleep. They never lost the tingling sensation and the pain at times was unbearable.

Sarah wore compression socks to help with the swelling. Still she could hardly walk sometimes. Over the past few months she had developed an ulcer on the pad of one of her feet.

Today she waited in an office reading a novel about a German spy in the First World War.

It was a book she picked up on her way out the door. She regretted not having a bookmark. Sarah tried to memorize her page number when the nurse called her name.

In a patient room she removed her shoes and answered some questions. The nurse helped her with her compression socks and told her Dr. Nathan would see her soon. She opened the book to the page she was pretty sure she'd read half of.

After a while Dr. Nathan came in and she sighed. Again she tried to remember the page number. He smiled awkwardly and asked if she was alright. Sarah shared her predicament with him and he laughed. Then reached into the pocket of his white doctor's coat and pulled out a business card.

Sarah beamed and was relieved to not have to remember the page number. It would be later in the evening before she'd be able to open the book again.

She glanced at the card and was surprised Nathan was his first name. Not that she could pronounce his last name. It looked to be somewhere between German and Russian. Regardless, Sarah was happy to have a bookmark and told him all about her foot ulcer.

Luggage Claim Check

Billy swore as he watched the luggage carousel. He had a green ticket with his bag number.

Finally after what felt like hours, he found it. The flight had been frustrating Billy since take off. Which was about the point he realized he had packed his book on his suitcase rather than his carry on. He had planned on finishing his last eighty pages on his short flight to Denver.

Then a thought had occurred to Billy. Perhaps he hadn't packed the book at all. It could still be laying on his bed at home. He tried to picture it in his head, that last look over the room before leaving. He could easily picture the book on the nightstand or on the bed. It was much too visual. He couldn't be sure until he opened the case.

Anxiety got the best of him. Billy hoisted his suitcase onto a nearby bench and opened the front pocket. There it was. Dead beat.

He really needed to know if Murphy's reputation would be salvaged and how Harry would deal with the Necro this time. He'd been addicted to the series since he'd picked up the first book a few weeks back.

Billy zipped his suitcase and carried the book through the airport. He tucked the baggage claim ticket at the end of the book, marking the last page. He contemplated the anticipation he had endured on the plane.

He knew he would finish it tonight. Billy couldn't wait.

Hearts

Dahlia cried for days after the death of her dog. He'd been around since she was in the fourth grade. She knew he'd lived a long life but she had selfishly hoped he would make it until she was out of college.

At school she saw a counselor who recommended she write to the dog about how she felt about his death and her favorite memories of his life. He had even given her a small piece of paper with two joined hearts printed at the top. It didn't have to be long, but she had no idea how to start.

Sorry you died? I miss you?

Nothing seemed right. Dahlia started after a few months to not be so sad about his death. It still bothered her that she couldn't find the words to write for him though.

She started keeping the slip of paper in a book and carrying it with her. Dahlia would walk to the river from her dorm room and try to read, though the paper often made focusing on the book difficult.

One day in late May, Dahlia found inspiration. She suddenly knew what she felt. In the book was the paper but she hadn't remembered to bring a pen on this walk.

She didn't want to lose it. Running, she turned for her dorm. She was almost there when she saw a dog in the middle of Broadway. Without looking she dashed to save it from the four lanes of cars. Tires squealed and Dahlia never saw the truck that hit her. She did see her dog though. Waiting for her by the side of the river.

Scrap

It had been 12 weeks since Cal had started working at the dentist office. The job was tedious, checking in patients and booking appointments. All paperwork went through him.

He felt like he was starting to get used to it. Making less mistakes and being less nervous answering the phone. He wasn't the only receptionist but the lady he worked with was on the edge of retirement and was teaching him everything. She drank her coffee black and smoked two Marlboros everyday on her lunch break.

Cal preferred to read on his. He ate a snack and sandwich from home most days and got into some fiction before he had to get back to work with his mentor. Today she had left him with a pile of paperwork that had to be shredded. Some of the pages he saved for scrap paper that weren't confidential, such as a few forms that had printed crooked. He cut them into fours and always felt very 'green' in doing so. He liked to use them by the phone for messages he didn't have to enter on the computer. Cal also liked to use them to remind his mentor when he would be. Ask from his lunch. She didn't need his help. He knew that, but he wanted her to know when he would be back to help anyway.

On his lunch break, today he was excited to start a new book. He had found it in the dumpster of his apartments and couldn't stand the idea of it ending up in a landfill. He decided that if he read the book it justified keeping it.

Usually he used a bookmark from the set his mother gave him at Christmas but he didn't like the idea that the book that had almost been destined for the trash would have his mother's bookmark. Cal decided that one of the quarter sheets of paper would suit better. Since they were also things he saved from the trash. He held the page with his finger until he made it back to his desk. This one had one quarter of the instructions for a program on the back.

Watching him, his mentor shook her head and answered the phone.

Index Card

The bookstore was more crowded than usual when Heather walked in. She'd forgotten there was a sale. Her journey to spiritual enlightenment was to be taken one step at a time.

She'd just finished the third and final book she'd purchased on zen. Still she had questions. Thus the bookstore on a busy sale day.

Heather perused the shelves on spirituality. There were so many options. Christianity, Judaism, Wicca. She'd spent a long time looking into all of them. Peace was her final goal. Zen Buddhism spoke quieter than all the others.

She'd read but the crusades where the Catholic Church fought to stamp out the Muslims in the beginning. She read about Jews being forced into camps during the Second World War. The burning of witches at the start of her country's history. Then about the peaceful life of modern day monks.

Heather considered the dramatic change in her life. Including the abusive relationship, she had spent the last year escaping. She treated him as he who should not be named. In group she talked about the brushes and the trips to the ER about the words that cut deeper than the punches.

Now she was on a journey to heal her soul. One step at a time. She found a few books that spoke on the history of dhalsim. How it spread through China and its effects on dynasties. Another on the life of Gandhi. A third of daily practices to heal the soul.

At the checkout she picked up a small package of index cards to make notes on as she read. She opened it on the bus home and placed them sporadically through the books.

Heather opened the first book and continued her journey to peace.

Envelope

They had been friends for three years. Tonight would be the first time Sebastian had spent the inside of his apartment.

The party was supposed to be a pretty big affair. Which really wasn't Sebastian's cup of tea. He just couldn't justify turning down an invitation. It was to announce an engagement of his long-time friend and his girlfriend. Debastian was happy for the couple. They suited each other. Parties on the other hand, involved conversing with people. Talking about what he does for work. Where he went to school. How he knew the couple. A fun story but not one he wanted to share on the night the engagement was announced.

They'd met on a dating app. Looking for a third none of them had a clear idea of what they wanted. They'd experimented and in the end, decided to remain friends. With occasional benefits. Recently they'd moved their apartment and Sebastian had expected to be invited for a game night or a movie. After a month, he thought maybe they'd just grown apart. Sad for the friendship, but it happened.

When he arrived at the apartment there were a number of people already crowding the small living room. His friends waved and introduced him to others.

After a while he found a book and a corner. There he started to read. A few times he was asked what the boom was. He showed the cover and joked that he was stealing it from the hosts. Then brushed off the conversation politely. Then suddenly his lap was filled with a beautiful twenty something man with drinks in his hands.

"You wouldn't look up from your book, so I made an entrance." Sebastian knew he was struck.

He set down the book open faced down to keep his place and leaned back to enjoy the enigmatic creature in his lap. Neither made a move to get up and Sebastian's heart raced when their fingers brushed in taking the offered drink.

When the night came to an end the mysterious man got off his lap to use the restroom. Sebastian tried to pick up the book but couldn't focus on any of the words. An envelope poked out from the back of the book and he used it to mark his place. He looked up to find his friends. They told him the mystery man didn't like goodbyes. So he could call him. If he wanted to pursue anything.

Sebastian ran outside. He could vaguely see a figure walking away. He chased him until he was close enough to be sure it was him and grabbed his hand. He looked into his eyes for a moment out of breath. The mystery man smiled. Sebastian pulled him close and kissed him.

Marika

Eden closed her book and stepped off the treadmill. She hated that her hobbies always seemed to be mutually exclusive. To everyone else, reading was something she felt could be done anytime or place.

What she hated more than the looks she got, stretching with a book in her hand. Was the chaffing between her thighs form the leggings she wore to the gym. Ede often got looks as a 'big' girl at the gym. Some people just didn't like to see unathletic bodies. Some people also had other opinions Eden was not required to care about.

She showered and changed. Ignoring the look from the older woman as she peeled off her sweaty sports bra and wrapped herself in a towel for the shower. After she decided the chaffing was too much and tossed her long loved leggings in the trash.

An hour later at the mall, she stretched and pulled as she tried on new pairs of athletic pants. She read in line at the checkout, and at the table at the food court as she chowed down on some Chinese food.

At some point she'd lost her bookmark and reached into the bag to pull the tag off her new leggings to use in its place.

Eden continued to read in another line and finally went home where she finished the book. Leaving the tag randomly between its pages.

5/11/2018

The cross country trip had been long so far, but Blake still had a few more states to cross before he'd be done, so far he'd read most of his book without stopping.

At a fuel station, somewhere in Idaho he decided he needed something to drink and to pee. Blake took the book inside with him. Purchased a few bottles of soda and asked to use the restroom.

That was where he realized he still didn't have a bookmark. He asked if the mega drew that night and bought two lines. Then he tucked it into his book, marking his place and found the restroom.

The next morning two states away, he looked up the numbers. It was a dud, but still, it marked his place.

Date Due

Fiona's daughter had been born out of wedlock and without a father. Her parents had disowned her for breaking the laws of their church. She'd lived for the last fourteen years as a single mother to a beautiful daughter. She would change a single thing.

Especially today. Over breakfast. Fried egg sandwiches her daughter had made on her own. She had casually told her she had a crush. Her crush's name was Melody and how do you know if a girl might like girls instead of guys?

At first Fiona had been shocked. Mostly that she had never guessed. Never wanting to think of her baby girl as anyone else's. She hadn't even considered sexuality as a part of her daughter's existence. Considering she hadn't known her own daughter liked girls she had no idea how to answer her question.

Instead, she asked how she showed she likes girls. All of a sudden she could see it. Her not at all sporty daughter in a ballcap. Rolled cuff sleeves. The consistent begging to chop off all her beautiful hair. To her daughter's credit she laughed:

"All signs point to gay, mom."

So now she was at the public library in the parenting section. Again. This time looking for books on how to support her child. Nothing could alter her love for her but Fiona knew they lived in a world where one isn't always free to make their own choices. A world that could shun its children.

On her way to the checkout she glanced over the books for sale and found a copy of *Now That You Know.* She bought it for a quarter. Fiona started flipping through while she waited outside the school to pick up her daughter. The bell rang and she pulled the due date folder from the front and used it to mark her place. A few minutes later she spotted her daughter holding hands with a girl.

"Hey mom. This is Melody, my girlfriend."

10% Discount

The winter of 2008 was colder for Saul than any winter he had previously endured. He was in his freshman year of college and a new student at BSU. The snow was amazing but the cold was terrifying.

He'd been warned about the extreme change from Georgias hummus state. Saul would need all of this finger to count the number of times he'd heard the phrase. *"Don't like the weather, give it five minutes, it'll change."*

That first morning of winter, he met her and it didn't matter to Saul if it was 95 degrees or four. He'd dreaded the solstice, lamented his roommate for making him come to another cause in the sub.

Saul didn't get her name. All he could do was obediently answer her questions Name? Saul

Age? 19

Major? Sports Medicine

She gave him a 10% discount to a food place, then turned to the next person. This heart stayed in his throat. As he watched her from across the scantily crowded room. He couldn't stop handling the card in his pocket. Careful not to bend it he ran his hand over its smooth surface.

An hour later the event had ended and he offered to help her clean up her table. He asked about the coupon. Good through June and the fast food place. She told him it was close to campus and she worked there part time.

Saul spent the following week trying to figure out the fastest ways to walk there. The greenbelt was pretty relaxing but the cold made him want a straight shot.

He carried the discount card in a warm copy of Dickens, hopefully she'd be there.

Sometimes he caught a glimpse of her ponytail in the kitchen.

Maybe one day he'd learn her name. If the cold didn't get to him first.

Dried Rose

Brenda had seen her favorite band twice and had met them once. That didn't stop her from buying tickets to see them again. Her date had backed out at the last minute.

Still Brenda would see them. She brought a book and made her way to the barrica. She didn't mind waiting in line or for the show to start. A few guys tried to talk to her about how she could read in a crowd.

None of the crowd is mine, she thought.

She read until the opener was ready to start. Enjoyed their performance and then read some more. Repeating until the band she came to see would perform.

Just before, a man to her right asked her if she had seen the movie that had just come out based on the first book. She had seen it. With the date that had stood her up. Still she enjoyed the discussion with a man who had already read all three books in the trilogy.

Towards the end of the set she had come for, her day started to catch up with her.

Brenda considered leaving early and beating the rush outside. She found doubt every time she convinced herself she would leave.

I can sleep when I'm dead
30 isn't too old to stay up this late

At the end of the set the lead singer threw roses at the crowd. Brenda caught one and was absolutely delighted in her choice to stay. On her way out she bought a hoodie and took a selfie with the rose.

Then she pressed it between the pages of her book and went home to bed.

Two Dollars

On a cool Saturday morning Henry set out random items on a fold out table. It was one of three set up in his driveway. His wife putted around him, adjusting or pricing things he would have rather taken to the thrift store.

He would have rather spent the weekend reading or working on the house, but it would be nice to have the garage back.

Since retirement, his wife had taken to purchasing storages and selling the findings. Sometimes she had him fix things or she painted and turned things into art. After a while he looked around and decided it was good enough. All he needed was a book and a place to set and read.

Henry went inside and hauled a recliner to set up in the garage. After finding the right space he looked around for a box of books he'd brought out. There were a few she had thrown in from a storage unit and he wanted to see if anything looked good.

He found a Coban novel and sat down to read. A few people drove by and stopped. It was early yet and his wife set up a table to paint at, in-between socializing with the neighbors. An hour or so in she decided to get breakfast and left him in charge. While she was gone he sold a man a light fixture for two dollars. She hadn't left Henry the money box so he tucked the two bills in his book and continued to read. When she returned he used the bills as a bookmark and dug into a breakfast burrito.

Halfway through the afternoon they covered up the tables and pushed the rest into the garage. Henry took his book inside if he didn't finish it tonight, tomorrow would be soon enough.

Leaf

September was a bittersweet month. It was beautiful and blissfully cool after the summer months. It also meant an end to summer shenanigans and getting back to school. Determined to make the best of it, Sadie took her reading under a large tree on campus. The leaves shook in the wind and fell around her. It was peaceful and suited the story perfectly.

Only halfway oblivious of the world around her she registered the extra presence under the tree with her. This was campus. On a Thursday between classes. Other people had a right to be around. Even if it was a rippling disturbance of her peace.

For a while she continued reading, then a hand was way too close to her face and on her hair. She looked up suddenly and found a girl. Close to her in age pulling a lease out of her long curly hair. Sadie was abashed to have been so surprised and quick to frustration at the stranger.

When she looked closer the girl was really pretty. She had red hair and freckles doting her face like constellations. Sadie wanted to find them all and never look away from her eyes.

The girl smiled and introduced herself.

"I like your pin." She said after and pointed at a rainbow pin on Sadie's collar. "I like your freckles!" Sadie, grinning, almost shouted back.

The girl blushed and then tucked the leaf in Sadie's book.

"Maybe I'll see you around." Then she was up and walking away. Sadie wasn't sure if it was what she'd said or how she'd said it that scared her off. But she jumped to her feet and ran after her. It was the most uncharacteristic thing she'd ever done when she pulled on the girl's hand and asked her for her phone number.

"I don't have a phone. I know it's strange these days but I don't want one. If it's meant to be, I'll run into you again."

Sadie didn't know why she wanted to cry. It was the best way to blow someone off, especially some random girl chasing you down for your number.

When she returned to her book, she couldn't focus on the words anymore. She decided to go back to her dorm and face the part of her day she had dreaded the most.

It had been nice having a room to herself. Almost four days without a roommate. Today she should meet her. If she was still lucky it wouldn't be a sporty girl or a girl that had a problem with her sexuality.

When Sadie unlocked her door she closed her eyes, wanting to savor the last few minutes of unknowing. To her complete surprise she was met by all her new favorite constellations. The beautiful redhead with freckles wasn't her roommate. She was her new roommate's sister.

The constellations moved when she smiled. Then the girl reached for the book in Sadie's hand. She flipped to the leaf serving as a bookmark.

"See, it was meant to be."

38 Cent Jackpot

Bonding wasn't really Graham's thing. When he'd agreed to the boys' trip to Jackpot the month prior he'd thought the plans would fizzle out. They usually did when his dad made 'boys' weekend' plans.

It all started in his grandma's kitchen. Graham had been there for some free food after work that he didn't have to cook himself. There wasn't anything new on his end. When he got there he'd been ambushed by his dad's unusual barrage of questions.

No he didn't have a girlfriend. Work was good.
His place was fine. He could afford food.
The Honda was still functioning.
He could take time off next month. Why?

He was given a noncommittal 'just curious '

Graham had his suspicions but decided it would fizzle out before he had to participate in a family function.

Unfortunately, his dad showed up at his job the next day. They talked over the time he could take off and Graham's boss had approved it on the spot. A boy's weekend the following month.

Graham didn't ask which boys or if it was just open to the men of the family.

Now he was in the back of his brother's minivan reading a book on his phone. He'd packed a physical book too but it had been getting dark when they'd finally got loaded into the car. He chose the way back for the extra room and the better chance of being left alone long enough to read.

Graham was one of four tall men making the four hour trip to the casinos. The other three were his dad, brother and whatever his brother's brother-in-law was to him. They'd all been coerced in the same way as Graham, but they seemed to like the idea of the trip better than he had.

When they got in the first thing they did was check into the hotel. After about half an hour they were ready to meet up and find a card table. The free drinks made it worth it, but Graham had to leave the book he'd fished out on a nearby chair.

He wasn't good at cards and decided to switch to slots. That at least he could have his book on him. After a while he won and then lost somewhere around fifty dollars. When he reached the last thirty-eight cents the rest of the boys had found him and wanted food. He cashed out and took his winnings slip, it would serve him better as a bookmark than as change in a book. At the restaurant he got a burger and fries to offset the drinks. He showed his dad his big winnings.

Laughing he marked his page again and took a grinning bite out of his burger.

Love This Author! Sad, But Interesting story :)

Gaels life revolved like clockwork. On Sunday she attended church, Monday and Thursday she bought groceries, and on Tuesday she went to the library. The check outs at the grocery store knew her by name. She bought what she called a ration of coffee and sugar.

Monday she bought flour and staples. Thursday she bought veggies and perishables. If asked she simply said it was the way her mind worked. She could only remember half of the store at a time.

She started every day at the bus stop by her house at 8:30, no matter the weather. In winter she wore a large purple coat she had kept for years. In the spring she carried a large red umbrella with happy faces. In the summer she wore jumper shorts. Always she had a backpack with her essentials. Wallet. Keys. Book. Drawing pad.

No matter the weather when the right scene struck her she would draw. Sometimes it was the rose garden, or Friendship Bridge. Sometimes it was a couple in an embrace. No matter where she was she would start a sketch.

At the library on Tuesday she would exchange two books for two more. Gael enjoyed reading. It was great for waiting for the bus and the ride across town to church. She tried to give herself at least an hour a day to read. Sometimes painting took over her time.

Last week she found a new book by an author she had enjoyed previously. Halfway through she'd had to stop to paint a portrait of a pregnant young woman alone at a train station. She finished the book before bed on Monday and ripped off a small piece of paper from a notebook. She wrote "love this author! Sad, but interesting story!" And tucked it into the pages for the next reader.

The next day she took the book back to the library and sighed heavily before putting it in the return box. She'd never been a mother. Her art had taken up so much of her life. Gael had married and quickly been widowed. The years following had been dark and her art showed the depressing side of love lost. It had been over forty years and she had never remarried. She bought a little house in the east end with the insurance money and spent her days the way she wanted. She hadn't needed children, or a husband. Only herself and the quiet peace that let her paint.

Ripped Piece of Page

On Wednesday, Kyle rode his longboard to school. It was the first clear morning in weeks and he was excited to get some practice. All week he had half days so he could practice at the park after.

When he got there it was clear he wasn't the only one with the idea of enjoying the warm day. Most of the park was full of parents with kids and a group playing basketball. Kyle rode around a few times and tried to flip his board, but it felt different on a longboard, and he fell. He skidded and scraped his arm from elbow to wrist.

Deciding he needed to take a break and let the nausea subside, he found a tree and got out his book. His arm hurt and he knew he would hear about it when his mom saw the blood on his shirt.

Looking at it made him sick but it would be fine when it stabbed over. He flipped open the book. Chapter seven was where he had left off. He tried to read chapter by chapter. If he left of in the middle he usually had to start over, or it would take the rest of the chapter to remember what had happened in the beginning.

A few chapters in he took a break, looked at the leaves on the tree above him. Felt the wind on his skin, now that it didn't sting his arm. He looked down at his book and the first sentence caught him. He was halfway through the chapter when the urge to look up struck him again. It was time to get moving. Time to board home.

Kyle looked down at his book realizing he was going to have to start the chapter over anyway. He ripped a piece of the last page off the book and placed it at his spot. It was one of the first signs he might be a psychopath, but no one saw it. He rode his longboard home. He still didn't land the flip but this time he caught himself before the ground could damage him.

In loving memory

July 25, 1959 - November 25, 2010

For fifty-one years Jodi had been a timid woman. She had loved her children. Obeyed her husband. Minded her parents. On the day of her death she made a quick decision. Rash and unethical. She had debated for days after if it had been the right thing to do.

Then she'd attended her funeral. Not as a ghost, but as her new self. Her face had been burned badly during the fire and she had taken clothes from the homeless shelter.

She hadn't known that when they found the body it would be mistaken as hers. Going to the funeral had been her plan to let her family know the body wasn't hers. To take their grief away. Then she watched. Jodi saw people drop flowers on her coffin. She saw the tears.

Listened to the I love you's and the stories about her life. The repeated 'she's in a better place' was the final piece to make her change her mind. They hadn't bothered to know her. She'd never wanted to peacefully let go.

Now Jodi had a new name. An under the table job as a fry cook and a small studio apartment with a small bookcase and a king size bed. Her closet was full of clothes she'd always thought for someone else. Too bright for her mother, too sexy for her husband. With her face no one wanted to look at her anyway. Why should she care what anyone thinks now?

After returning home from work, the woman who was no longer Jodi, took a shower and climbed into bed. On her nightstand was a stack of books she'd been meaning to read, all stacked waiting their turn for her attention. It was the start of her weekend. She could read late tonight. It was too bad her eyes felt heavy after a few chapters. She opened the drawer of her nightstand and felt around for a bookmark. Her hand fell upon a small card that would work. On one side it had a beautiful sunset. The other had a bible verse, under her name and the dates of her life. In loving memory.

She thought for a second about her children, the new grandchildren she'd seen announced online. Then stuck the card between the pages of her book. They would live a life they chose to live. Just as she had for so many years, and would for as many more as she had left.

I Love You a Folded Page

Antony watched his girlfriend as she read on the couch. He'd been playing a game and got up for snacks. It was a rare weekend they could share together. One or both of them usually worked or had some other engagement they needed to attend. From the small island in his kitchen he could see her profile as she read. The way she looked reading was one of the first things that had attracted him to her. The way her face gave away her emotions. How her lips would sound out words she wasn't sure about. The way she would try to make expressions of characters.

    He wasn't sure if she was trying to snarl or curl her lip while he watched, but it was adorable how she looked. Antony cut up a few apples and grabbed a jar of peanut butter. She was still reading when he spooned some into a bowl. Next to the fridge was a stack of paper he used to leave notes for himself. He glanced at her again and was struck with inspiration.

    Antony took one of the pages and folded it into fours. On the inside of the last fold he wrote "I love you". He hadn't told her yet. Their relationship had been long enough for it to be appropriate, but he'd never found the right moment. He put the paper under the plate of apples and brought their snack to the couch.

    Sitting across from her he entwined his legs with hers in the middle seat. Leaving the plate and bowl on the table in front of them. She looked up and smiled. His heart skipped, like it did when she smiled at him. Then she jumped up and announced she had to pee. He laughed and then sighed when she left her book in her vacant seat. Antony snuck the paper from under the plate and found the last page of her story. He placed the paper just after so he wouldn't ruin the ending for her.

When she came back, they ate apples and peanut butter. She told him how she liked the book and complained about the main character making stupid choices. Then they went back to playing games and reading.

When his hand started cramping from the game, he took the dishes into the kitchen and looked through the fridge for something for dinner. He threw out a few ideas and she gave some non-committal grunts in response. It was usual when she was getting to the end of a book.

Eyeing the few pages she had left made him grunt. The closer she got the more nervous he became.

Antony gave up on wanting to cook and ordered Chinese food. He wouldn't have to cook and there wouldn't be a lot of dishes. Spending a day gaming and relaxing with his girl sounded like the best way to finish the day anyway.

After a while he was submerged in the game again. It took him a little to realize she was sitting still, with the book closed in her lap, staring into space. Nerves took him again. Maybe she didn't want to know yet. Was it too soon?

"How was the book?" He asked. She didn't respond. When he glanced there was no sign of the paper, maybe it was still in the book? Had she closed it without finding it?

"She left it on a cliffhanger, I didn't know it was a series. I'm not ready for this." She told him after a few minutes of him sweating.

"OH!" he exclaimed. He had to think fast. She wouldn't find it if she didn't open the book again. Then he would have to find another way. Nervous again he tried, "Maybe there is a little bit from the next book after. Did you check?" She sighed.

"I can check." When she opened the book, she flipped through to the end, finding the last page she reread it. Then she turned the page.

Antony didn't know if he should watch, or look away. If she would look at the paper she now held in her hand. He watched her move it to her other hand looking puzzled. Then she flipped through the rest of the blank pages. .

"Nothing else. Funny I didn't think I used a bookmark..." She trailed off as she opened the paper and read. "Was this you?" She held her breath and met his eyes.

Antony nodded. He couldn't trust his voice, he didn't remember how to breathe. Before he understood what was happening she was in his lap kissing him and laughing.

"Do you mean that?" She asked and he nodded again. "Say it then! Tell me what it says!" "I love you," he breathed, starting to realize her reaction was a good one.

"Again!"

"I love you," he said again, smiling.

"I love you, too. Took you long enough to say it though. I thought I'd have to be the crazy one and say it first." She kissed him again.

Antony didn't know why he'd waited either. But it had been almost as nerve racking as trying to build up the gal to ask her out.